NORMAN'S FIRST DAY
AT DINO DAY CARE

Written and illustrated by Sean Julian

North
South

Miss Beak's play group was warm and welcoming.
"Good morning, everyone," said Miss Beak.
"This is Norman. He's joining our group today."

But when all the little dinosaurs looked around
to say hello, they couldn't see Norman anywhere.

"Is Norman an invisible dinosaur?" asked Freda.

"Norman's not invisible,"
Miss Beak replied.
"He's just a little shy."

"Don't be shy! Just say hi,"
said Jake in such a big booming voice that the ground shook.

Everyone was used to Jake's loud voice. All except Norman, of course, who had quickly hidden among the pencils. He was good at hiding.

"Maybe today we should use our indoor voices," said Miss Beak.

As the other little dinos played,
Norman watched from a safe place.

Norman was amazed at how confident
the other little dinosaurs seemed. He wanted
to join in the fun too, but he didn't know how.

Right then . . . a ball bounced toward him.

"Maybe this is my chance to join in," thought Norman.
He ran and kicked the ball with all his might.
   To Norman's surprise the ball flew through the air—
over Rodney, over Jake, and over Zoe—until it landed
with a splat, right in the middle of the swamp.

Norman was very embarrassed.
He quickly went and hid.
He was good at hiding.

At lunchtime everyone sat in a circle.

"Why don't we all say what we did over the weekend," Miss Beak suggested.

The other dinos talked happily, but for Norman it was a very scary thing.

So when it was Norman's turn to speak, he . . .

. . . hid under the cushion.

After lunch Norman looked for a quiet spot and
started stacking some pretty pebbles.
It was normally a game he played by himself.

But someone was watching.

"That's amazing," said Tina. "You're very clever."

Norman wasn't used to the attention, and he didn't know what to say, so he quickly scampered up a tree.

"I really want to join in, Miss Beak, but I feel shy."

"It's okay to be shy," Miss Beak replied. "It's a special part of who you are."

"Really?" said Norman.

"Absolutely," Miss Beak replied. "And I wonder if this afternoon we can discover what other amazing qualities you have hidden inside."

Miss Beak split the class into pairs and asked them to perform something for the group.

Zoe and Rodney wanted to play music. Tina and Freda both loved to dance.

Norman was very worried about performing; in fact he was about to run and hide. But then he noticed something surprising.

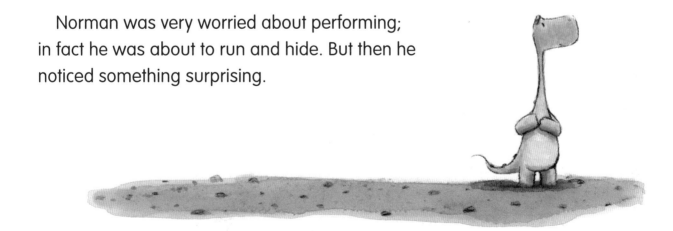

His partner, Jake, was looking worried too.
"Are you okay?" asked Norman.
"Not really," said Jake. "The idea of performing makes me feel shy, like my stomach is full of wriggly worms."

Norman was surprised. **"But you're so big!"**

"It doesn't mean my fears are small," replied Jake.
They both giggled, and for a moment they forgot
about their worries.

"Maybe together it'll only be half as scary," said
Norman. But neither of them knew what to perform.

Miss Beak opened the dress-up box.
"Maybe you will find an idea in here?" she suggested.

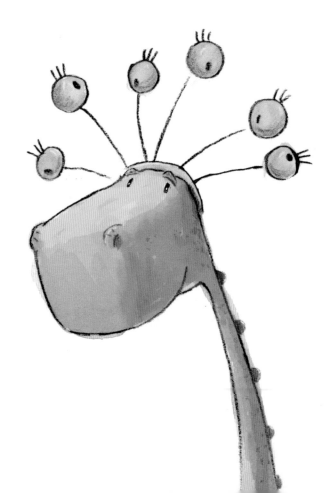

They tried on lot of things—

and had lots of fun—

until Norman had a magical idea.

After Zoe and Rodney played their music and
Freda and Tina performed their dance, Jake slowly
walked onto the stage to perform a magic act!
All by himself.

"Where's Norman?"

Jake was feeling nervous, but he knew something that no one else did.

Jake took off his hat and gave it a tap with his magic wand.
To everyone's astonishment and delight Norman magically appeared from his hiding place inside the hat.
He really was good at hiding.

There would always be a part of Norman that was shy, and he was okay with that. Because now he knew that hidden inside himself there was also courage, and he would always have his friends to help him find it.